Rumpus Rc

CW00847510

written and illustrated by
Heather S Buchanan

edited by Nina Filipek
designed by Liz Auger

Published in Great Britain by World International,
an imprint of Egmont Publishing Ltd., Egmont House, PO Box 111,
Great Ducie Street, Manchester M60 3BL.
Printed in Finland. ISBN 0 7498 2274 0

A catalogue record for this book is available from the British Library.

N
W E
S

Basil Bat's branch

Rumpus Rabbit's burrow

Muzzy Mouse's house

Maurice Mole's hole

Scampa Squirrel's tree

Henrietta Hedgehog's log

Buttercup Meadow stretches from the Deep Dark Wood in the north, where Basil Bat and Scampa Squirrel live, to the small stream in the south, where Maurice Mole has his home.

Henrietta Hedgehog lives in an old log on the east side, and Muzzy Mouse's straw house is under the hedge to the west. In the middle of the meadow lives Rumpus Rabbit.

This is Rumpus's story...

T he sun was streaming into Rumpus Rabbit's burrow when he woke up early on his birthday.

"Today is a very special day!" he thought. "I must do something today that I will remember forever."

After breakfast Rumpus set off for the little stream which ran through Buttercup Meadow. He loved to play beside the water, making dams and waterfalls and getting really wet.

Rumpus noticed several fallen branches beside the stream, and this gave him an idea.

"Why don't I make a raft?" he asked himself. "A present from me to myself to have an adventure with!"

So he began to tug the branches to the edge of the water, and he joined them together with some string he had found caught in the ferns. He made the raft wide enough for him to sit on. Then he added a mast, and tied his old red-spotted handkerchief on to it, for a sail.

It looked wonderful!

R umpus moored the raft by anchoring it to a big tuft of grass.

He bounced up and down with excitement. All he needed now was some food to take on board before he set off on his adventure.

"Adventures always make me hungry!" he said to himself, as he hurried back to his burrow.

B ack at his burrow, he found all his friends waiting for him. They smiled and waved. And they had presents for him.

"Happy Birthday, Rumpus!" they called.

Rumpus was too excited about his raft to notice the presents. "Come and see what I've made!" he called back. "You won't believe your eyes!" He picked up a large carrot and a dandelion cake, and led his friends back to the stream.

O ff they went, Rumpus bounding ahead, with Muzzy Mouse, Scampa Squirrel, Maurice Mole and Henrietta Hedgehog puffing and panting behind. Basil Bat swooped along just above them.

"We can go for a sail!" said Rumpus.

"Do you know all about boats then?" asked Maurice.

"Oh, yes. I've always wanted to be a sailor," said the rabbit.

B ut when they got to the bank,
Rumpus's raft was nowhere to be seen.
Poor Rumpus was horrified. His raft had
floated away down the stream, having
slipped free from the tuft of grass. The
animals could just see it in the distance.
"What can we do?" wailed Rumpus.

Everyone dropped their parcels on the bank and rushed into the water. All except for Basil Bat, who flew swiftly overhead and was first to land on the raft, and Rumpus and Muzzy, who both shouted directions from the grass.

Suddenly in all the commotion Rumpus, who couldn't swim, overbalanced and fell into the stream.

R umpus went under the water again and again.

"Help!" he gasped, each time he came up.

The raft was safe with Maurice Mole and Basil Bat now.

Henrietta Hedgehog and Scampa Squirrel swam back as fast as they could to save Rumpus. They laid him gently on the bank while he coughed up lots of water.

Poor Rumpus.

"What a way to spend my birthday," Rumpus thought.

"Well, Rumpus," said Scampa Squirrel. "I'd forgotten to bring you a present, but now I know just what you need. As soon as you feel better I'll give you swimming lessons. You can't be a sailor if you don't know how to swim, can you?"

The raft was tied up beside them now.
Maurice lit a fire to warm Rumpus,
and the rabbit began to open his presents.

A woolly sweater from Henrietta
Hedgehog. A basket of dandelion heads
from Maurice Mole. A pair of red running
shoes from Basil Bat. And, last but not
least, a lovely new handkerchief from
Muzzy Mouse.

They all had some dandelion cake and carrot, and sang 'Happy Birthday'. Rumpus felt better, and smiled. He thanked his friends for everything. They had given him wonderful presents, saved his raft and, most important of all, they'd saved him from drowning.

Then Scampa taught him to swim. All the animals held him up whilst he kicked and splashed and spluttered.

When he could swim across the stream seven times without stopping, and dive in off the bank, they all cheered.

"Now we can go for a sail!" said Rumpus excitedly.

Basil sat at the back with Scampa, who used her tail as a rudder. Rumpus stood proudly by the mast with Henrietta and Muzzy, and they sailed into the sunset. Maurice fell asleep in a little heap because he was exhausted.

The raft sped along as the dew fell on Buttercup Meadow. Rumpus said it had indeed turned out to be a birthday that he would never ever forget. And everyone agreed!